BooBoo

Olivier Dunrea

HOUGHTON MIFFLIN HARCOURT
Boston New York

To access the read-along audio file, visit
WWW.HMHBOOKS.COM/FREEDOWNLOADS
ACCESS CODE: SNACK

AGES	GRADES	GUIDED READING LEVEL	READING RECOVERY LEVEL	LEXILE® LEVEL
4–6	I	F	9–10	320L

www.hmhco.com

The text of this book is set in Shannon.
The illustrations are ink and watercolor on paper.

The Library of Congress Cataloging-in-Publication Data is on file.

ISBN: 978-0-618-35654-6 hardcover
ISBN: 978-0-618-75505-9 board book
ISBN: 978-0-544-31363-7 paperback reader
ISBN: 978-0-544-31362-0 paper over board reader

Manufactured in China
SCP 10 9 8 7 6 5 4 3 2 1
4500499899

For BooBoo

This is BooBoo.

BooBoo is a gosling.

A small, blue gosling
who likes to eat.

BooBoo likes to eat from
morning till night.

Every day.

In the morning she eats
everything in her food bowl.

"Good food," she says.

BooBoo visits the hens
and gobbles their grain.

"Good food," she says.

BooBoo visits the goat
and pokes her bill into
the trough.

"Good food," she says.

BooBoo visits the mouse
and nibbles from his dish.

"Good food," she says.

Every afternoon BooBoo
goes for a swim in the pond.

She tastes the weeds.
"Good food," she says.

BooBoo is a curious
blue gosling.

Who likes to eat.

One afternoon BooBoo
saw bubbles floating
over the pond.

She opened her bill
and swallowed
a bright blue bubble.

"Good food," said BooBoo.

Then she burped.

She burped forward.

She burped backward.

She burped under water.

She burped in the weeds.

"Drink water!" said the turtle.
BooBoo guzzled and
gulped water.

She burped a teeny
tiny bubble.
"Good food," she said.

BooBoo is a gosling.
A small, blue gosling
who likes to eat.
Almost everything!